Welsh

Stargone John

Welsh

Also by Ellen Kindt McKenzie:

• • •

The King, the Princess, and the Tinker
Illustrated by William Low

Stargone John

ELLEN KINDT McKENZIE

ILLUSTRATED BY WILLIAM LOW

A REDFEATHER BOOK

Henry Holt and Company · New York

Library of Congress Cataloging-in-Publication Data
McKenzie, Ellen Kindt.
    Stargone John / by Ellen Kindt McKenzie ;
    illustrated by William Low.
    (A Redfeather book)
    Summary: Six-year-old John, emotionally withdrawn and resistant
    to traditional teaching methods, experiences ridicule and punishment
    at his one-room schoolhouse, until an old retired teacher reaches
    out from her blindness to share with him the world of reading
    and writing.
        [1. Emotional problems—Fiction.   2. Schools—Fiction.
    3. Teachers—Fiction.   4. Blind—Fiction.   5. Physically
    handicapped—Fiction.]   I. Low, William, ill.   II. Title.
    III. Series
    PZ7.M478676St   1990
    [Fic]—dc20   90-34119

    ISBN 0-8050-1451-9 (hardcover)
    10 9 8 7 6 5 4 3 2
    ISBN 0-8050-2069-1 (paperback)
    10 9 8 7 6 5 4 3 2 1

First published in hardcover in 1990 by
Henry Holt and Company, Inc.
First Redfeather paperback edition, 1992

Printed in the United States of America
Recognizing the importance of preserving the written word,
Henry Holt and Company, Inc., by policy, prints all of its first editions
on acid-free paper.∞

• • •

For my aunt, Ruby Hill Wons
E.K.M.

To Amanda
W.L.

Contents

Stargone John

The boy's plain star gone

Trouble for John

"The boy's plain star gone," Ma said, and tugged John forward. Her voice was as loud as when she has her dander up, so everybody in the classroom heard her words. I knew right off there was trouble waiting for John.

I truly wished Ma had let me bring him. I could have explained better about John. Shy the way he is makes him special to me, because I'm the only one he really talks to. That means I'm bound to look out for him.

But Ma had said, "John's being how he is, I'm obliged to bring him." So she had.

The new teacher looked hard at John and said, "What do you mean, 'star gone'?"

"He don't think the same," Ma told her. "It would be more fit for him if he could sit by his sister till he gets accustomed to school ways."

"Who is his sister?" the teacher asked.

I put up my hand, and then slid out of the seat and stood up as polite as I knew how. "There's room by me for him, ma'am," I said.

"Miss Vordig, if you please, when you address me," she said. She picked up a paper off her desk and looked at it. "Sit down, Liza Bain. You are in an upper grade. John is just beginning. He will sit here. Sit down, John," she ordered him, and pointed to a seat in the first row.

John didn't lift his eyes up and he didn't move. I could tell how tight he was holding to Ma's hand. It would take some prying to get him loose.

"Stargone John!" I heard from behind me, and a snigger to go with it. It had to be Bradford Cronis, who I truly hated, and I knew I'd have to kick him come recess. That meant he'd pull my hair, but I didn't care. I'd kick him hard enough to make it worth the while.

"Sit down, John," Miss Vordig said again, and from her voice I had the sense of an iron chisel froze in the ground in the snow-cold of winter.

When John still didn't move, all at once Miss Vordig had him by the shoulders and jerked him around and sat him down so hard I knew it hurt. She did it so fast, I don't think either Ma or he knew how it happened. Ma just stood straight.

"You may go now, Mrs. Bain," Miss Vordig said. "I'll handle him."

I knew Ma had to be respectful to a teacher. Still and all, I wished she had explained it different about John. I would have liked it if she'd argued for John to sit by me, or even taken him back home with her. I truly hated it that she just turned around and walked out without saying a word.

John sat real still. He didn't move an ear. I could only see the back of him, so I couldn't tell where he was looking, but I figured straight ahead the way he does. You don't know what he's seeing when he does that, because his eyes don't look at what's in front of him. I almost felt like crying for him.

John wouldn't cry. He never cries, so nobody could call him a crybaby. That would keep Bradford Cronis from saying I had a baby for a brother. I was shamed for thinking that because John was brave, I'd be saved a teasing.

Miss Vordig was looking at the paper on her desk again.

"Bradford Cronis," she said without looking at him. "You will stay in at recess and write fifty times on the board, 'I will not speak out of turn.' "

I kept my mouth real still, even when it tickled to turn the corners up. But I was mad too, because now I couldn't kick him, and by lunch I'd probably not feel so much like doing it.

I was right about that. There was so much to bother over that morning that by noon I'd clean forgot about Bradford Cronis.

I agonied over John and how it must be for him, sitting next to Helen Wick's little sister Jane. I agonied over Ma calling him star gone and saying he thought different. If she'd only said he took in more and said less, it would have made more sense. Besides, calling him star gone was only a family doing, and now that Bradford Cronis had picked up on it, that name would stick to my brother forever. I agonied over my not arguing more with

Ma to let me bring John myself so as I could explain about him my way.

While I was thinking all of that, I got in trouble with the reading because I wasn't looking at the words in the book. I kept stumbling over them until Miss Vordig changed my place and made me sit with the third-graders. That was awful. It put me back in the second reader. I could read real well, and I could spell and cipher too, just about the best in the class.

"Guess your head don't hold any more than a wet stocking holds water!" Alice May said to me at recess. She'd been peeved all summer about my doing four points higher than her on our report cards last spring. Now she turned up her nose like she didn't want to have anything to do with somebody who was put back in the third grade.

"I got more important things to think about," I said to her back, and walked over to kick stones off the edge of the school yard into Mr. Crawley's parsnip bed.

I wanted to be where I could watch John at recess, but Miss Vordig was making him sit in his place because he hadn't done a thing she'd told him all morning. So there he sat. I was feeling plain frantic because she hadn't let him out. I knew he'd ought to go, and I tried to tell Miss Vordig so.

"Miss Vordig," I'd said, "you'd ought to let John . . . "

"Sit down, Liza Bain. John is not your affair."

Well, what do you do, as Pa says when he can't figure out the way to do a thing. You wait till you know. So I waited. When she kept him in at lunchtime, I knew there'd be a disaster. It happened. John wasn't a corked-up rain barrel. He sat there still as ever, but we could all hear what was happening. Miss Vordig turned pink in the face. Her nose got pinchier and she sucked her cheeks in farther than ever.

"Fetch the mop, Liza Bain," she said. "And you, John Bain. You go home."

"He don't know the way," I said without asking permission to talk, or saying Miss Vordig or ma'am or any of it.

"Then you take him home, Liza Bain, and see to it that tomorrow nothing like this happens."

But it was her fault! I took John's hand. "You should have let him relieve himself," I told her straight out.

Ma would be peeved. It was Monday—wash day—and she and Katy would have been stoking the wood stove and carrying water from the bay to heat in the big copper boiler and wringing the sheets and rubbing out collars and elbows and hanging up clothes all day long. When we got home, Ma would stand the way she does after she's done a morning of weeding or hoeing or chopping wood—or spent the day at the washboard. Her back curves in and her chest pushes out and her hands rest on the back sides of her hips, thumbs forward and elbows back. Katy would be short tempered, and here I was bringing John home smelling of wet pants.

"You should have learned your ABC's," I grumbled at him.

He didn't say a word to me. Then I stopped worrying about him, because I remembered that it being wash day, Ma would have left all the black stockings soaking. It was my job to rub them out with soft soap when I got home from school. The water would be cold and slimy. I hated doing those stockings worse

I couldn't tell what he had in mind

than poison. I kicked a rock and scuffed the rest of the polish off of my shoe. I hated those shoes anyway. Last year they were too big and this year they pinched my toes.

"You do better tomorrow," I told John.

John rocked along beside me with his legs stiff and kind of far apart the way you do when you have wet pants, and I couldn't tell what he had in mind.

The Meesong

The next day wasn't any bit better, except for John got to go out to the privy.

"I'll show you where," I told him, and took him out back at recess. I hoped he'd get along all right, because he wasn't used to a three-holer with boys he didn't know being around. I waited, and then brought him back because Miss Vordig was making him sit in his seat again.

"You all right?" I asked him at lunchtime, after I took him again. I saw to it he rinsed his hands and then fetched his bread and apple. He had to stay in to eat his lunch.

The third day, Miss Vordig was standing in front of John and tapping her hand with her ruler. All at once she said right out, "Liza Bain, is John able to understand what he's told?"

"Yes ma'am, Miss Vordig," I said.

"Is he able to talk?"

"Yes ma'am, Miss Vordig." I tried to answer same as she asked. That is, without caring one bit whether he could or not, just wanting to know.

"Then he'll learn," she said, and reached down and took John's hand and hit it real smart across the palm with the ruler.

I could feel tears come to my eyes for knowing how that stung and I blinked hard, but John didn't make a peep.

"John, you will sit there until you make the letter A." She pointed to the slate and slate pencil in front of him.

John sat.

I hated Miss Vordig worse than wolf bait. I figured right then how I'd run away with John and hide him in the woods or, better, in the bear cave up in the bluffs on the bay side of the point. I'd bring him bread and milk every day before school and after school. I thought how we'd talk together. I'd tell him all about what was happening at home—how it was with the horse and the cow and the kittens and whether Bagley had met up with a skunk or maybe a porcupine and had to have the quills pulled out of his nose.

John would talk to me. He'd tell me about . . .

"Liza! Liza Bain! Are you as star gone as your brother John? Answer me this minute!"

I could have answered right if I'd known what Miss Vordig had asked.

So while I stood in the corner and hated Miss Vordig all over again, I got to remembering Miss Mants from last year and wishing she was still here. She'd been the teacher here a long time. Katy and William and Leland and Caddie and Martha had

had her before me. I'd had her since I started first grade. She'd gotten pretty old by the time I was through the third grade. I suppose that was why she'd gotten peculiar.

That's what people said, anyway. George Gotock's daddy said, "Cora Mants has got peculiar. She thinks too much and speaks out too free about what she thinks. Who knows what she's learning them? Time we had a new teacher for the school."

Ma and Pa had laughed at that. But I guess others went along, because we got a new teacher. Miss Vordig.

We'd been glad, I guess. I remembered about last spring when we would change seats with each other if Miss Mants didn't have her glasses on. She'd look at where we should be and call our names, but we'd be on the other side of the room and everybody would giggle. We knew we weren't being respectful, but it seemed real funny to us. We figured we knew more than she did.

But now, like I said, I wished she was here instead of Miss Vordig. With Miss Mants we'd learned to read and cipher. We sang songs and drew pictures. I listened when she told the fifth- and sixth-graders about history and geography. That's why I know about the Greeks and Romans and George Washington. That's how come I know just where we live on that peninsula that sticks out in the water with Green Bay on one side and Lake Michigan on the other.

None of it had seemed so special at the time. But while I stood there and looked at the cracks in the wall and how they went slantywise up to the ceiling, I thought maybe it had been special after all. I couldn't remember George Washington sounding so everlasting dull as Miss Vordig made it. I couldn't ever remember Miss Mants cracking a ruler over a first-grader's hand because he couldn't make a letter A. But I couldn't remember how she'd gotten us to do it. It seemed like I always knew.

I did remember how she'd read a story to us first thing every morning. That is, she used to read. Last spring she would just tell it to us. I guess she knew them all so well, she didn't have to read them anymore. I liked Miss Mants all right, except her eyes had a funny milky look over them that made me uncomfortable as to whether to look at them or not to look at them.

But like I said, even George Gotock learned to make his ABC's, though his daddy said he wouldn't have any use for it. His daddy didn't see where anybody had any use for it except for the town clerk, who had to know how to write down where the property lines were and who got married or born or died. George Gotock's daddy said, "What else good is it? I don't have a book in the house. I haven't read anything in twenty years and I get along fine."

Pa said as how ignorance was the scourge of the world and no child of his would grow up without learning to read and write.

Charlie Blue Hat, who helps Pa out now and again, agreed with Pa. Charlie can't read, but he says a man who won't learn his own people's way isn't worth a cold stone for frying fish. Charlie didn't much admire George Gotock's daddy.

I can read, like I said, but I can't read all the books we have at home, especially the big one called *The Decline and Fall of the Roman Empire*. I take it down every now and again to see. Pa only went through third grade, but he'd read that book. He read

The Sentinal when it came out once a week. All of the goings on from all around. Aloud. Pa said reading was important. And what Pa said, went.

"Listen, John," I said when we went home after school. "You have to learn your ABC's because it's important. And it can't be that hard to do."

"It has to be good," John said, soft the way he talks to me and watching his feet.

I knew what that meant. John meant it had to be worth the while.

"It is good," I told him. "But if Miss Vordig can't teach you how, I'll take you to the bear cave. You can stay there so she won't hit your hand."

John was real quiet. The bear cave was special. Uncle Lute had told us about it. It all started with the stars. We were looking at the Big Dipper in the north sky one night. It's a regular soup ladle of stars. But Uncle Lute told us as how the ancient Romans called it the Great Bear and showed us how it made a bear instead of a dipper. Then he told us how on cloudy nights the bear would come down and stay in the biggest cave up on the bluff above the bay—the one you couldn't get to. I knew Uncle Lute was just telling a story, but John and I still talked about how it would be to meet a bear made out of stars in that dim, dark cave.

After a while John said, "The Meesong will be in the cave too."

The Meesong was something only John knew all about. When he just sat and didn't look at what was in front of him, I figured he was thinking about the Meesong. He'd first told me about it when we were playing bear cave under the table. All those big people's legs were walking around the kitchen and all their talking was going on over our heads, and he told me soft how the Meesong was his special friend. It was about as big as he was and knew everything and could do everything. It took him everywhere it went, so John knew everything it knew.

The Meesong hid behind the couch and listened to how we did things. Then it went and did those things itself.

"Only the Meesong does them better," John always said.

When Bossie went dry, John told me the Meesong's cows never went dry. When the Hutchers' barn burned down, he told me the Meesong's barn never burned down. When Annie Cross's baby sister died, he told me the Meesong's babies never died. The Meesong brought in enough wood so its house was always warm no matter how deep the snow was or how hard the northeaster blew.

When John and I went down to the harbor to look at the fishing boats, John would say that the Meesong's fishing boat always came back with a good load of fish, or that it never got caught in a storm, or that it never sank.

The Meesong crept through the high grass and learned how the Indians did things too, only the Meesong did them better.

"It can tiptoe through the woods without wiggling a single leaf," John said. "It can bring down a deer with one arrow, even if it's not big."

John told me it knew how to make clothes from the deerskins, only they were softer than the Indians made them. "Soft as cat fur," he said.

He was star gone, and now and again he got whacked

It knew how to weave porcupine quills into its moccasins for prettier designs than even the Indians made. "All bright and ripply like the bay under the sunset clouds," John told me.

It made baskets that held water and dried blueberries, and the bugs never got in them. Its canoe never leaked, but floated on the water still as a red maple leaf with its edges curled up. The fish would jump right into the boat.

The Meesong was special just between the two of us, and I was fairly honored he told me about it—so I had to agree with him.

"Yes, I expect the Meesong will be in the cave," I told him. "I expect the Meesong knows the Great Bear."

"I'll live in the bear cave too," John said. "I'll live with the Meesong all the time."

"All right," I told him, "as soon as I find a way to get there. Then you'll learn to do everything the way the Meesong does—better than anybody else in the world. Even the ABC's."

Of course I didn't have time to hunt for a way to the bear cave. I figured he knew we really *couldn't* get to it, but it might help him try to learn his ABC's if he thought the Meesong could.

But John didn't learn. He didn't even try. He came with me every day because he was small and he had to, but he just sat there. He sat and didn't talk. He sat and didn't read. When Miss Vordig spoke to him, he sat. I don't think he heard her. He was star gone, and now and again he got whacked.

That first week was pretty awful.

An Idea That Might Have Helped

The second week John let Ma know he wouldn't go to school.

There was a real ruckus about that. I got in the middle of it when I said how Miss Vordig whacked him. Ma's mouth got thin lipped and tight together.

Pa said, "If it takes a whacking to get him to know his ABC's, he'll have to get whacked."

I allowed as how it wasn't doing him any good toward learning.

Pa said, "If you're looking for a good tanning for being so smart mouthed, young lady, I'll see to it."

I knew he wouldn't whip me. He let Ma do the punishing with us girls. But it put me to feeling on the outs. When John and I left for school, we were both in a bad mood.

"I've a mind to start looking for a way to get up to the bear cave right after school," I told John. "I'll stay there too."

When we were settled at our desks, I got to wondering if John thought the bear in the cave would be a real bear or would be stars with spaces between them. It would be too bad not to see the bear when somebody as awful as Miss Vordig could stand there plain as day. That put me in the corner again for not paying attention to the subtraction.

I stood there thinking how if there was anything I wanted to subtract, it was Miss Vordig. She called on Alice May, and I heard Alice May do the right numbers in that smarty voice of hers. Alice May could say things back once she'd learned them, but she could never figure anything out on her own. I watched a little spider crawling down the wall and wondered why it didn't use the crack like a road. It would have been more fun to watch if it had. Then I started thinking about Miss Mants again.

I don't know why I only thought of Miss Mants when I was standing in the corner. Maybe that was when I had the time for it. Anyway, I thought that Miss Mants could have taught John how to make a letter A without ever hitting him. I thought she could have taught him to read and write and cipher and know and do everything better than anyone else, just like the Meesong John told about.

Right then and there I decided to go to Miss Mants's house and ask her how to tell John to make the letter A. In fact, I'd take John with me. We'd do it today. It might make us a little late getting home, because her house lay ten minutes the other way from school, but that didn't matter. I couldn't wait to ask Ma's permission. This had to be done right away.

I thought about it until Miss Vordig said I could sit down at my desk. She called on me to read right away and I did. I was so excited about asking Miss Mants that I forgot about hating Miss Vordig, and I read real well. I knew that book anyway. I'd done it last year.

That day was forever until school let out. It didn't matter quite so much that John had to sit in for recess and lunchtime. It did worry me that his ears got so red when his hand got whacked that afternoon, but I knew he'd be all right after we'd talked to Miss Mants.

When Miss Vordig rang the bell, I took John's other hand and we left the schoolyard.

"We're not going home, John," I told him. "We're going somewhere else."

The way he looked at me, I knew what he was thinking and I had to disappoint him a little.

"How could I find a way to the bear cave while I was standing in the corner? But I thought of a place where everything will be good."

When we got to Miss Mants's house, I noticed there were weeds in her flower bed. Ma weeds our flower garden clean. I knocked on the door.

I knocked again, and then I heard Miss Mants's footsteps, kind of slow.

"Who is it?" she called before she opened the door.

"Liza Bain," I told her.

"Liza Bain! Why, how nice," she said, and opened the door. "Would you care to come in?" She held open the door and stood against it. She looked older than I'd remembered.

"This is John," I said. "He's my brother."

"Hello, John," Miss Mants said, and sort of nodded to me.

"Say hello," I told him, but he pushed close to me while he stared at Miss Mants and didn't say a word.

"He doesn't like to talk much," I explained.

"That's all right," Miss Mants said. "There's people who talk all the time and don't say a thing."

I didn't see how that could be, but laid it up to Miss Mants's being a little peculiar. Right then I wondered if maybe my idea was wrong. But here I was and I'd better be polite.

"We come for a visit," I said, and since a visit called for more talk, "John just started school this year," I told her. "That's why you didn't know him from before."

"Come in and sit down, Liza and John," she said, and motioned us in.

There wasn't much else to do but go in and sit down. John came along without any fuss. The room was dim and dark after the bright sun, and it was a minute before I decided which end of the sofa to sit on. I picked the end by the table. John sat beside me.

"I believe I have some cookies in the kitchen," Miss Mants said.

She moved off kind of slow, with her hand out to touch the doorjamb when she went through to the kitchen.

I looked all around. The table by the sofa was round, with a marble top. We had one almost the same. Ours was between Pa's and Ma's chairs, only there was a crocheted doily Aunt Abi had made on it, and a lamp, and Ma's mending basket full of stockings. Pa sat by the lamp to read in the evenings.

I was feeling more and more uncomfortable

Miss Mants's chairs were all pushed against the walls. One had a little square table beside it. That didn't have a lamp either. There was a bookcase chuck-full of books. There was a spider-web in the corner of the top shelf. There was a desk beside the other door. There was a barrel stove, but of course there wasn't any fire, being a warm day in September. I wondered what to talk about. I was feeling more and more uncomfortable. John sat by me and didn't move.

Miss Mants came back with a plate of cookies. She put her free hand against the wall and rubbed it all the way to the chair where the square table was and put the plate down there.

"Help yourselves," she said, and rubbed her hand along the arm of the chair before she sat down.

I felt real strange about getting up to go and take a cookie.

"No thank you, ma'am," I said, trying to be polite even if I wanted one. I wondered why she hadn't put them down on the marble-topped table beside us. But John got up and crossed the room and took one and ate it. He stood beside Miss Mants and took another cookie and ate it. I guess he was pretty hungry.

Then he surprised me past all thinking by asking Miss Mants a question.

"Why do you feel the wall?"

"Because I can't see, John," she said.

A Visit with Miss Mants

Well, that did it for me. If I'd had second thoughts about her being peculiar, I knew now that there was no way Miss Mants could help John. It made me almost want to cry. Then John surprised me again.

"What can't you see?" he asked.

"I can't see anything," Miss Mants said. "You close your eyes, John, and that's how it is for me." She didn't sound all sad and sorry for herself. She just said it out straight.

John closed his eyes. He reached out for the cookie plate but couldn't find it, so he peeked and then opened his eyes all the way and took another one.

"I guess he's pretty hungry, Miss Mants," I explained, in order to apologize for his taking three. "Miss Vordig took away his apple this noon."

"Why did she do that?" Miss Mants asked.

I told her. Once I started, I told her more than ever I intended. All about how John was really smart but nobody could tell because he wouldn't talk hardly at all or learn his ABC's.

"He don't get much chance to talk at home," I explained, "because everybody else is always talking. Pa says you can't get into a conversation with a knife blade and the words flattened to slip in sideways. I guess John just got in the habit of not trying."

Then I told her about my being put back into third grade. What I couldn't believe afterwards was that I even told her about the Meesong. I allowed as how John told me about it because I never laughed at him for what he said the way other people did.

"Why I really came for was to ask you to teach John how to make his ABC's," I said at last. "But you're stone blind, Miss Mants. You can't help him at all, and I'm truly sorry."

Miss Mants listened to everything without saying a word. She sat there a minute after I'd finished, and then she said, "Which hand did she whack, John?"

John held out his hand. Even in that dark room I could see it was red and puffy. Miss Mants held out her hand. "Put it in my hand, John, so I can feel it." John gave her his hand, and she touched it real gentle.

"Liza, you go through that other door to my bedroom and look on my dresser. There's a little jar there that says Lilac Cream on it. You bring it here and we'll see if it's soothing."

I felt shy about going in her bedroom, but I did. I found the jar and I looked around at where her nightgown was hanging on the bedpost and how the wardrobe had a leaf design on the door.

She talked to him like he was grown up

Then I brought the jar to her. She opened it and smoothed some of the cream on John's hand. You could smell the lilac scent of it right away.

"If you don't want to learn to read, that's your business," she said to John while she was doing it. "I expect you have a reason for it." She talked to him like he was grown up and not just six going on seven years old.

"It's no good," he said. "That's why."

"That may be," she agreed. "But I'm glad Liza can read, because there's a different jar just like this lilac cream, only it would have made your hand sting worse than another whack. Does it feel better?"

John nodded his head and stared at his hand and then sniffed it. "How do you know what it says if you can't see it?" he asked.

"I used to be able to see it," she told him. "Now I can tell it by the scent. You might say some of my seeing is in my nose. But most of my seeing is in my head from what I remember. Help yourself to another cookie, John."

John did. He didn't eat it right away, though. He stood there for a time with his eyes big and round as pie tins. I knew he was pretty excited about something.

Miss Mants and I talked about a lot of things after that. I told her about how Mr. Logan had his leg crushed when a log rolled on it at the lumber mill. She told me how Pete Peterson came and brought in the winter wood and split kindling for her.

"I had Pete Peterson in school twenty years ago," she said. "He was full of mischief at the time. But he was a good boy too. Now he's a fine man."

John didn't say any more. He had another cookie. He had six altogether and I had three.

Somewhere along the visiting, Miss Mants asked, "Do you ever draw pictures, John?"

I answered yes for him when I remembered Miss Mants couldn't see him nod.

"He draws dogs and cats real good, Miss Mants. He draws Bagley and puts his spots on him and everything."

"Maybe he'd like to draw Bagley while you and I are visiting, Liza. There's paper on that desk by the bedroom door. I don't have any colors for him, but there's a pencil. He can sit there or at the table by the sofa."

I found the paper and pencil and settled John. Miss Mants asked me about Ma and Pa and Katy and William and Leland and Caddie and Martha. I told her about *The Decline and Fall of the Roman Empire* and how I figured once I read it, I'd be smart as Pa. Then I wouldn't have to be in Miss Vordig's room anymore.

Miss Mants nodded and said, "That's so. Just as long as you knew what it said by the time you finished it."

Miss Mants truly had a way of saying peculiar things.

By the time we'd finished visiting, John had made a picture of Bagley. He brought it over and showed it to Miss Mants.

"I'm sure it's a very good dog, John," Miss Mants said. "But I can't see it."

John looked at her as if she'd just told on him.

She went on talking. "But there's a kind of way I can see it. Liza, you look in the drawer of that same desk. There's a little box with pins in it. Bring a straight pin here and I'll show John how I can see his dog."

I wondered if she was being peculiar again, but I had to find out how she could see John's dog with a pin. So I found one for her.

"Now John," she said. "You take this pin and make little holes all around the edge of the dog right on the lines you drew. When you poke the pin in the paper, it'll make a little bump on the other side. I can rub my finger over the row of bumps and feel how that dog looks, just as if I were seeing with my fingertip."

John knew right away what she meant, and he did a whole row of pinpricks around that dog. It took quite a while. Miss Mants and I visited until John brought it to her.

"Turn the paper over and put your finger where the nose starts," she told him, and then she put her finger where he showed her and rubbed very gently all around the outside lines of the dog.

"It's very good, John, and I'm pleased to know you can draw so well. But you know, there's one thing. A wolf and a dog look a lot alike. A fox and a cat might look a lot alike if you were feeling around a row of pinpricks. Now if I were deaf as well as blind and couldn't hear you say that this was a dog, I might think it was a wolf. So I'm going to ask Liza to print 'A Dog' underneath this picture. Do it in big letters, Liza, because I want John to make pinpricks in those letters so I can feel them."

I did what she said and when I was through I handed John the paper.

"That first letter is A," I told him.

John didn't say anything. He put his head down and began to make pinholes in the paper.

When he was through, Miss Mants didn't turn the paper over, but held it flat up and rubbed her finger underneath the letters. "I do it underneath this way, because if I turn it over, it's backwards. It says 'A Dog.' "

She appeared real pleased that she could read it.

When we left, Miss Mants said as how she was glad to catch up on all the doings of the town. She said she didn't get out much, and now that Pete Peterson had a wife and baby, he didn't always have the time of day to pass with her. She said we should come again anytime we liked.

We didn't get home till supper. Ma said I'd have to go to bed without any, but being it was Monday, I had to rub out those black stockings first.

Where's John?

We didn't go to Miss Mants's after that. We were to come straight home after I was out of school at four o'clock, with no dawdling on the way. In school John still didn't do any learning. He just sat. And got whacked.

"That brother of yours truly is star gone," Bradford Cronis said to me, and I chased him so I might kick him, but he ran too fast.

The first- and second-graders got out earlier, so John waited for me at the rope swing. He was always there when I got out. Until one day in October.

It was a day that started off wrong from the minute we got to school. Bradford Cronis did it. He said, "Here's Stargone John again, just waiting to get hit!" Then he yelled:

"Liza Bain, Liza Bain,
Stands in the corner come sun or rain!"

I held my temper. When that didn't fetch me, he went on:

"Stargone John, Stargone John,
Don't know his left shoe to put it on!"

That was more than I wanted. I went after him. But like always, he ran faster than I could. He turned around ahead of me and yelled, "Nyah! Nyah! Liza Bain, got a pain!"

When Miss Vordig rang the bell, I had to give up chasing him. But I was in such a fury that when we lined up, I got out of line and walked over and kicked him so hard on the shin that he yelled a different tune. I got a shaking and had to sit outside the door all morning. Then Miss Vordig made me stay after school. Usually John had to wait an hour and a half for me. Today he had to wait two.

When I got out, he wasn't there.

"Where's John?" Ma asked right off the way I knew she would.

I was out of breath and hot and scared and ready to cry.

"I don't know," I told her. "He didn't wait for me the way he's supposed to. I looked and looked and looked, and then I came home because I couldn't find him. I thought maybe he'd be here."

Everybody started looking for John. First we looked all around the house and yard and barn. We called and shouted and hunted. Then Ma and Caddie and me went down to the harbor because we knew how John loved the boats and the water. It was scary to think maybe he'd fallen off the dock and drowned. Ma and

He yelled a different tune

Caddie asked everybody, but nobody had seen him. I guess you could hardly expect those big fishermen to notice one little boy.

From there we went to Mr. Clement's store. Mr. Clement's store had everything you could think of—pickles and dry goods and pins and soap and licorice. It was the candy that made us think John might be there. But Mr. Clement hadn't seen him either. Of course, he might have missed seeing him, because John's head doesn't come above the counter and he wouldn't have said anything.

We didn't go to the lumberyard because Pa was going there to look. William and Martha were to ask Mr. Crawley and everybody else near around the school. Katy and Leland were to hunt the road that went off to Egg Harbor.

We asked all around town—even people on the street—but nobody had seen John.

Finally we started for home.

"Did Miss Vordig hit John's hand with the ruler today?" Ma asked me.

"I don't know," I said. "Maybe."

It was hard to say because my throat hurt the way it does when you swallow too fast. That was because I knew for sure that John had run away and would never come back. This is why. When we'd gone to school in the morning, he'd said to me, "If she hits me again, I'm going to live with the Meesong." And I just now remembered it.

Ma asked, "Don't you know if she hit him?"

"I was out of the room for a time. I didn't see."

Now I could hardly see anything for my eyes blurring. Tears

turned everything colored the way the frost on the grass had done this morning. Only the frost had been prettier. It sparkled all gold and green and red and blue, prettier than Ma's glass beads. Just this morning John told me the Meesong gathers up the sparkles and stitches them to its clothes so it's the shiniest thing in the world. That was why the sparkles never last long in the grass. I thought as how my brother thought of things nobody else ever did.

The frost was beautiful to look at then, but now all I could think was how cold it was. All I could think of was John out in the woods, running away through the cold night and looking for the Meesong. He might even try to get to the bear cave. That made me more frightened than before. I've known forever that the Meesong was something John made up, but I wasn't sure if John knew. He talked about it like it was really there. If he'd run off to find it, we wouldn't find John until he was stone-cold dead with white frost on his jacket. Thinking about it made me hurt all the way from my chin to my belly.

John's being dead was all Miss Vordig's fault.

I had to run to keep up with Ma, she hurried so for home.

When Ma and Caddie and I got there, Leland and Pa and Martha and William and Katy were all there too.

So was John.

Ma reached for him, and I wasn't sure whether she was going to hug him or shake him. She decided on shaking him.

"Where have you been?" she asked in her loud, dander-up voice. "Don't you ever run off like that again! We were about to have the whole town turn out looking for you!" When she got through shaking him, she asked again, "Where have you been?"

John didn't answer.

"He says he's been to a bear cave," Leland said.

Seemed to me there was the scent of lilacs in the room, but that couldn't be, because it was October.

6

A Dog and a Cat

It took two days before John would go back to school. He wouldn't ever have gone except Pa talked to Miss Vordig. Then Pa told John that Miss Vordig wouldn't hit him anymore, but he had to go and sit there every day and not be a bother. So John sat. Miss Vordig put a slate and a slate pencil in front of him, but he never used it. He just sat.

That is, *Stargone* John sat. Because by now everybody in the school called him Stargone John. Even the other four first-graders, who should have been his friends, called him Stargone John. Helen Wick's little sister Jane was worst of all.

I didn't like Jane almost as much as I didn't like Bradford Cronis. Whenever Miss Vordig punished Bradford, I was glad, because even when he didn't deserve it, he deserved it. But Jane Wick never got punished for anything. She never did anything wrong. And I had to admit she was pretty smart, smarter than Alice May, who was more "smarty" than smart. Whenever Miss Vordig called on her to read, she read the words right. Whenever

Miss Vordig called on her to print words on the blackboard, she spelled them right.

Whenever Miss Vordig called on John, he just sat. After a while she stopped calling on him. Seems like she got to where she didn't notice him anymore at all.

But Jane Wick noticed him. At recess she would say, "What's the matter, Stargone John? Can't you spell dog? It's D-O-G, that's what it is."

Sometimes she said "cat" and sometimes she said "baby." John would walk away. Sometimes the older boys would jump in front of him so he couldn't help bumping into them, and then they'd say, "What's the matter, Stargone? Are you so star gone you can't even see where you're going?"

I'd get so mad, I was in trouble one day after another. I spent more time standing in the corner than I did sitting at my desk. I made mistakes reading the easy-reader because I was so mad, I couldn't bother to look at the words. Then Miss Vordig made me sit with the little second-graders. That was awful, because the seats were so small, I had to put my legs in the aisle.

The teasing got worse for both of us. They started calling me Lazy Liza. Bradford Cronis was first to do it.

> "Lazy Liza and Stargone John,
> They don't know what's going on."

I got mad enough I wanted to cry. The other boys picked up on it until there just got to be too many of them for me to kick. Besides, I was tired of being in trouble all the time. When reports came out, Ma and Pa would find out about what had been happening. Maybe Pa would whip me. Add to that, I began to wonder myself if John couldn't understand things.

"I wish you'd learn to make your ABC's, John," I said one day when we were walking home. "I wish you'd learn to read and write. It would sure save me a lot of trouble."

"The Meesong can do it," he said, "better than anybody."

"That's fine for it," I said, stopping and putting my fists on my hips with my fingers curled up the way Ma does—not when she's tired, but when she's mad. "But it don't help me one bit. I'm plain tired of fighting and being called names and standing in the corner all day. I'm going to end up dumb as a cow."

John stood still and pushed the toe of his shoe around, making circles in the dust.

"There's other things the Meesong likes better," he said.

"Like what?" I asked.

He pushed his toe around some more. "What's good," he said after a while, and wouldn't say any more.

All I could do was puff the way Ma does when she's plain put out with Pa. That happens when he says, "If it's not good, it's not worth the while." And she doesn't know if he means good for fun or worth the effort or just good for nothing.

The next day I 'tended to the easy-reader. It was so boring, I wanted to yawn out loud. I looked over to where John sat. He was leaning over his slate and making marks on it with the slate pencil.

"What are you scribbling, John?" Miss Vordig asked, and Jane giggled.

Miss Vordig picked up the slate and looked at it.

"Hmmp," she said. "Well! Look at this!" She held it up so we could all see it. It was a picture of Bagley. I knew it was Bagley because there was that shaggy look he had, with his ears one higher than the other and bent over just at the tips. There was all that hair around his eyes and his tongue hanging out. It was a better picture of him than I'd ever seen.

Everybody stared at it.

At the bottom of the slate John had printed "A Dog."

I was so proud of John, I was ready to shout.

Then Miss Vordig said, "I suppose we should be grateful. It's only three days before Thanksgiving and John has learned his first word." Then she took up the eraser from in front of the blackboard and wiped the slate clean. "Let's see if he can learn to print 'cat' by Christmastime."

She put the slate back down on his desk. Nobody laughed but Jane.

I felt plain wretched at seeing the picture go. But John started making marks on the slate again. When he finished, it was lunchtime. As we filed out of the room, I looked at the slate. There was a picture of a cat on it, and at the bottom of it he had printed "A Cat."

It seemed to me everybody filed past John's place and looked at his slate.

Bradford Cronis said in a kind of low voice, "Yay Stargone!" It was like a cheer, and I didn't feel the least obliged to try to kick him.

When we came back after lunch, the slate was wiped clean again. John didn't say anything. He just went at it again without ever paying any mind to what Miss Vordig was saying to the rest of the first-graders. He worked at it until half past two, when it was time for them to go home. When Miss Vordig took the first- and second-graders out, Mary Jaklee, who sat behind John, reached over and picked up the slate. It went around the room. There was a really good picture of Bagley again, only this time he had a fat stomach. John had printed "The dog ate a cat."

By the time Miss Vordig came back, John's picture was back at his place, and we had all stopped laughing. She picked up the slate and looked at it. I thought she'd be pleased, but she turned pink, like she does when she's peeved.

"Hmmp!" was all she said. She didn't offer to show us. She just wiped the slate clean.

Some Surprises

Whatever Miss Vordig thought, once I knew John could make his letters, I didn't worry about him. People mostly stopped teasing him, except for Jane. She kept after him on and on.

"Why don't you ever learn another word, Stargone John?" she'd ask. "Can't your head hold no more than five?"

Some days later, during the first-graders' learning time, Miss Vordig said, "Everybody's had a turn but John. John, go to the board and at least write a word."

Everybody in the room picked up on his name and watched. I held my breath.

John got up kind of slow and went to the blackboard. The other first-graders had put something out of the reader there. Some was spelled right and some wrong. John took up the chalk. I didn't know if he'd draw a picture or what.

Jane whispered, loud enough for everyone to hear, "Do you suppose he can print his name? B-A-B-Y."

*Everybody in the room picked up on his
name and watched*

But John printed real neat: "JANE IS BAD."

The whole room sort of exploded. You can figure how pink Miss Vordig got. She took John's arm and hustled him out of the room, and I heard her say, "And you sit there the rest of the morning!"

He was still there at lunch. After lunch he came in and sat down and didn't say anything or do anything. But he had a look on his face I'd never seen before. I got the feeling from it that he figured he'd evened things up with Jane and Miss Vordig both. And there was something else in it that made me think maybe there were things the Meesong showed him how to do that he hadn't told me about. It made me feel a little peculiar.

Anyway, I figured that was the end of it and now John would read and print like everybody else.

It wasn't, though. And he didn't.

Everybody still called him Stargone, though it had a different sound about it, and nobody jumped in front of him or yelled verses at him anymore. But he wouldn't draw or print on his slate at all. Miss Vordig didn't ask him to either. It came to me she might be afraid he'd print something she didn't know about. In no time she stopped noticing him again.

As for me, I was still sitting in a little second-graders' chair. I sat there until Sally Brody tripped over my feet and fell and got a bloody nose.

After that I was allowed to sit with the third-graders. It was more comfortable, but I had to sit beside Annie Cross, who I didn't like very well. Besides that, I was bored beyond reason, so I went to Miss Vordig. It was past Thanksgiving by then and

I thought she might be in a forgiving spirit. I knew if I was still in the third grade by Christmas, Ma and Pa would find out and give me what for.

"I hope you've learned your lesson, Liza Bain," Miss Vordig said. "But you're so far behind now, you'll have to stay with the third grade and do the fourth grade next year."

That made me see red as beets, because I did all the third-grade work in two minutes. The rest of the time I'd listen to the fourth-graders. I'd listen to the fifth- and sixth-graders too, and seventh and eighth besides, because when the fourth grade was writing or reading, I still didn't have anything to do. What's more, it wasn't yet December, so I wasn't that many months behind.

That day I went home with my stomach feeling like the inside of a butter churn.

I didn't sleep much that night, and in the morning my head was aching and my eyes hurt. It was hard to swallow the oatmeal, even with maple syrup on it. I went to school because I didn't want any notes passing between Ma and Miss Vordig. By recess time I felt plain awful, and by lunch I didn't want to get out of my seat. When Miss Vordig came in from seeing the first- and second-graders off, I told her I was too sick to stay another minute. I just had to go home.

I guess I must have looked sick, because she said there was something going around and told me I was excused. I put on my coat and hat and boots and went outside.

John wasn't at the rope swing. I didn't know where he was. I felt so bad, I didn't care. I figured by now he must know the way, and if he didn't, that was too bad.

When I got home, Ma asked, "Where's John?"

"I don't know," I said. "I want to go to bed."

She felt my head and tucked me in and sent Katy off to look for John. I went to sleep and had those funny, swirly dreams. When I woke up, it seemed like it should be morning, only everybody was having supper and John was there. He must have been in the privy when I came out from school. Ma gave me beef broth in a cup, but I don't care for beef broth. I went to sleep again.

I was real sick with a fever. After three days Charlie Blue Hat's wife came by with some bark for Ma to steep into a tea for me. Ma wasn't against using Indian remedies. Charlie Blue Hat's wife was special. She'd helped Ma through childbirth and Ma never lost a baby. Charlie Blue Hat used to say, "It's a good thing everybody doesn't love the same woman. They'd all want my squaw."

So I had to drink the stuff. It was bitter, but the fever went down.

When I went back to school, John was still sitting and not saying anything or drawing any good pictures. He was more star gone than anything I could think. He had to be spending all his time of day with the Meesong. I wondered I couldn't see it sitting beside him!

That's when things seemed the most hopeless I'd ever known. I was with kids younger than me, and I always would be. I knew all the stuff from last year, but now I'd missed two weeks of what the fourth-graders were doing, so I really was behind. When Bradford Cronis teased me, I didn't chase him. I didn't care. I hardly cared about anything. There wasn't any fun in it. There wasn't any reason for any of it. I might as well wash black stockings the rest of my life for all the good school was. I truly wished I could be out of there. But now I'd be in Miss Vordig's room for five years beyond this, instead of only four. I didn't know if I could bear it. I plain hated everything and everybody.

One day after school I said to John, "It's just no good." I hoped for John to tell me about the Meesong so there'd be something different to think about, but he didn't say anything. So I asked, "How's the Meesong?"

"The Meesong is busy doing everything there is to do in the world," he said, and sounded so sure of it, I almost believed the Meesong was real. But no matter how much I asked, he wouldn't tell me any more.

When I thought of it, he didn't say much of anything at all these days, and I didn't blame him. I only felt bad that he was keeping the Meesong all to himself and didn't want to tell me about it.

Then Christmastime came. At school we made Christmas cards and cut out snowflakes from folded paper and made colored-paper chains for our Christmas trees. We turned in all our readers and had a party the last day before vacation. Everybody had drawn a name to exchange presents. I drew Amy Clement's name. Amy Clement had lots of things, on account of her daddy had the store. I knew she had a doll, and I'd made a nightgown for it out of some flannel scraps Ma had. Martha helped me put a little crocheted edge around the neck and the hem. It was real pretty, and it almost cheered me to make it. I wished I had it for myself. I hoped if it didn't fit her doll, Amy'd give it back.

Amy looked at it and said, "That cloth came from my daddy's store."

Annie Cross drew my name. The Crosses were real poor. I went to their house once and was shamed to see how little they had. Annie and her sister didn't do well in school. They always smelled as if they needed a wash. I tried to keep a distance from Annie, but as I said, Miss Vordig had her sit by me.

When I opened my present from her, it was a bar of homemade soap. It didn't have any scent, except to smell of pork fat. I was going to be polite, of course, and say thank you, even if I was real disappointed. Then I saw that Annie had carved the corners round and made a sort of flower picture in the middle of the bar. I expect her mother had kept the shavings to use. I looked sidewise at Annie. She was holding her present. It wasn't a thing to play with. It was a jar of pickles. I guess somebody had thought the Crosses would like to have pickles. I saw that Annie's eyes were big and I could tell there were tears just under the lids waiting to spill out.

All of a sudden I knew she'd worked as hard to make that soap look nice as I had to make that doll nightgown. Maybe harder— for her. And I knew people seldom spoke kindly to Annie. All at once Annie got sort of mixed up with me being put back and John sitting and Christmas and I felt truly sorry about the whole world. It surprised me the words came out to say something of what I felt.

"Thank you, Annie. You made it so pretty, I don't know if I should use it or just keep it to look at." She had such a smile for it that I knew I wouldn't mind so much anymore that she sat next to me.

When the party was over we got together our peppermint candies and presents and paper chains and all our school papers. We got into our coats and boots and hats and scarves. I pulled the mitten string even through John's coat sleeves and helped him button up. Mikey Thorpe had given John a penny pencil with a rubber top to it. That was all John had to carry.

We were almost home when somebody yelled at me.

"Liza! Hey, Liza Bain!"

I looked around. It was Bradford Cronis. He was running after us.

I couldn't guess what he wanted. I hoped it wouldn't take long, because I'd gotten snow inside my boots from walking in the drifts and my ankles were wet and cold. Still and all, I waited for him, ready with a kick just from habit.

"It's not fair you should have to stay in the third grade," he started right out. "So I took one of our readers when Miss Vordig wasn't looking."

I remembered it was Bradford who put them away in the cupboard with the lock on it.

"It's a kind of worn one, but it's got all the stories in it. We're on page ninety-three. You could read up to that over Christmas. You can show her how you can read it when we go back. Only give it to me when you're through, so I can say it got mixed in with my papers." He handed me the book.

I couldn't guess what he wanted

When I couldn't think of anything to say, he said, "I don't like Miss Vordig. She's not fair." He turned around and ran back to where Billy Durette and Hank Troons were waiting for him.

I stood there with my mouth hanging open.

Christmas

Christmas is a good time. There was the smell of the balsam Pa cut and stood in a bucket of wet sand in the parlor, and of the cookies Ma and Katy and Caddie were baking. There was wrapping and tying, with Martha holding her finger on the knot for me and me holding my finger on the knot for her.

John asked for some school paper from me and if he could use my colored chalks. I let him use the broken ones. He busied himself. He'd lean forward and cover up the paper with his arm when I walked by. He didn't want anyone to see what he was doing. I figured he was making pictures for Ma and Pa.

There was that good feeling of secret surprises. All of it pushed out thoughts of school, though I did read some in the book Bradford gave me. It wasn't hard. I'd heard all the readings up to page fifty-seven. But I couldn't think much of reading just before Christmas. I'd have plenty of time to finish that book afterwards. I began to feel real cheerful. As far as I could tell, Miss Vordig hadn't sent home any note about me and John not doing well. There would be two weeks yet before reports came out. When I showed her how I could read that book, she'd have to let me back into the fourth grade.

Two days before Christmas it grayed up in the late afternoon, so it was dark by half past three. Then it started snowing big, soft flakes, the beginning of a real northeaster. It snowed all night. In the morning the flakes were small and coming down thicker than hasty pudding and blowing sideways fit to kill. You could hardly see the rail on the porch, let alone the barn.

Pa and Leland had to milk the cow and feed the horse.

"The other rope is in the barn," Pa said. "I'll have to take down the clothesline from the cellar." He did, and tied it to the porch post to take to the barn. He wanted to be sure they found their way back to the house.

When they came back, their coats and stocking hats and eyebrows were covered white. They stamped the snow off their boots on the porch and hung their coats behind the wood stove.

"There's no going anywhere today," Pa said.

"There's no need to," Ma told him. "We got all the fixings right here."

In time the house smelled of wet wool along with everything else.

Christmas morning our presents were hanging on the tree. I got a doll from Ma and Pa. It had a china face and a cloth body. Martha had sewed a nightgown for it just like the one I'd made for Amy. Caddie had knitted socks for it. Katy had made it a dress, and Leland had made a little three-legged stool for it to sit on. William had bought some blue tin doll dishes with flowers painted on them. I knew he'd spent his work money at Mr. Clement's store for them. I was never so pleased in all my life.

"I've never seen a prettier pot holder. Thank you, Liza," Ma said to me. "Did you make it all yourself?"

I told her yes.

Pa was pleased with the boot scraper. "When it thaws in the spring, I'll set it in the ground right beside the porch step," he told me.

Caddie and Martha and Katy liked the balsam sachets I made them, and I showed William and Leland how I'd nailed the two little dowels to a board and painted it. "It's for setting your mittens on to dry," I explained.

For John I'd bought a box of colored chalks.

With my colors John had made a picture of Bagley for each of us. Under each one he had printed "A Dog" with his penny pencil. Ma and Pa were real pleased with what Miss Vordig had taught him. I knew he'd taught himself by watching, but it didn't seem fit to tell them, or to tell them that John had only ever written "ate" and "cat" besides the words "A Dog" and "the." Running wolves wouldn't get me to tell them about "Jane is bad."

Outside, the snow still went on, but we didn't care. There was a fire in the stove, and the Christmas tree was bright with popcorn and cranberry strings and tallow candles. Pa played the dulcimer and we all sang. You couldn't want anything more cheerful, what with the smell of smoked goose roasting.

At dinnertime Martha and I set the table with the best plates. Pa and William had hunted the goose. Charlie Blue Hat had brought the wild rice and cranberries. Ma had given him some jars of cherry preserves. The squash and beets and pickles were from Ma's garden. John and Martha and I had picked the blackberries, and Katy and Caddie had bottled them. Ma had made the mincemeat with venison from the deer Leland had brought down. Something in that dinner was from every one of us. It was a nice thing to talk about while we ate it.

About four o'clock Christmas afternoon the snow let up. A good thing too, because the drifts were high as the chicken-coop roof and came up over the top step of the porch to mound up against the door. Now the wind had come around to the west and the sky was clearing northerly. We all knew what that meant. Stars would be out tonight big and bright as the beacon on the point. Tomorrow would be as cold as if the North Pole came south and sat on us. It was surely pleasant to be there warm and full and helping clear away the table and scrape the dishes and put away the leftovers.

About then Mr. and Mrs. Schlaag and Minnie came across the snow to the door. They're our closest neighbors. Mr. and Mrs. Schlaag came on snowshoes and pulled Minnie in a little wooden sleigh with a curved back on it. Minnie was wrapped up so you'd never know there was anybody in there, except for her eyes.

"We just couldn't let the day go by without we said merry Christmas," Mrs. Schlaag said as she and Mr. Schlaag took off their coats and boots. She'd baked a stollen, which she usually made for Christmas-morning breakfast, but it had been snowing too hard to come over yesterday, so she brought it for tomorrow.

Caddie gave Mrs. Schlaag the tin of cookies Ma had packed, and Ma brought out the second mince pie and the rest of the blackberry pie and started another pot of coffee. I showed Minnie my new doll.

Mr. Schlaag said, "Is a nice break in the weather, but Cholly Blue Hat says there's worse coming after tomorrow. So we stay in again so we didn't got lost."

Charlie Blue Hat was right about the weather. But somebody did get lost.

John Draws Another Picture

First, though, Leland got sick and then John got sick. Leland got better fast. I guess he just ate too much. But the night after Christmas John had the croup, and Ma was up until morning with him. That day he stayed in bed, and the day after that John couldn't talk. I don't mean he wouldn't, I mean he *couldn't*.

He did feel better, because he got up and padded around in the wool slippers Katy had crocheted for him and the bathrobe Ma had sewed for him. We sat together on the settee and looked at the picture book with rhymes in it that William had given him. He liked that book, especially the page with a picture of a bear in a cave. He pointed at the picture and tried to say something but nothing came out. That's how I knew.

"What are you trying to say, John?" I asked.

But of course he couldn't tell me.

"John can't talk," I told Ma. She made a mix of vinegar and honey, but it didn't do him good. I got to thinking then that he hadn't said much of anything other than to ask for paper and my colored chalks before Christmas. It came to me that since Thanksgiving he'd not talked in the mornings when he got up, nor at supper, nor when he went to bed. He'd gone and come from school without hardly a word to me, and what with my own troubles, I'd noticed but hadn't paid any mind. It struck me now that he was more star gone than ever, and nobody'd paid any mind at all.

The snow had started again, just the way Charlie Blue Hat had said it would. It had snowed for three days, just as hard or harder than before, so you can think how deep it was when it finally stopped. Pa had to go out through the upstairs window onto the porch roof and drop down to clear away the door before he could open it. He and William and Leland shoveled away so much snow, it looked like mountains on the sides of the path they made to the barn.

They'd just come in from milking, with their noses and cheeks all red, when Mr. Schlaag came across the snow on his snow-shoes.

"I didn't come for to stay. Because were you hearing about Pete Peterson? He went out three days ago for something and he wasn't coming back yet. Inger Peterson is so afraid he lost his way and maybe froze. People are going to look for him."

"Oh dear," Ma said, the worried way she does with three fingers on her lips.

"I'll help look for him," Pa said. "Does Ingrid have any idea where he was going?"

"No," Mr. Schlaag said. "She told he just got up all at once and said, 'By golly, with Billy being sick, I forgot,' and grabs his

Pa had to go out through the upstairs window

coat and out he goes, so fast Inger couldn't ask for what. It wasn't snowing quite so hard when he was leaving, but soon it really comes down. Inger doesn't know was he forgetting something at work. So everybody looks by the road to the lumberyard."

Pa shook his head and went for his coat. "He'd have gotten lost three steps from anywhere in that blizzard."

Leland and William got their coats and scarves and hats too. While they buttoned up, Ma asked Mr. Schlaag if Billy Peterson was still sick.

"Ya," he said. "There's lots of sick going around. Seems everybody got it but Minnie."

John had left off drawing pictures of Bagley with his new chalk colors. He got off his chair and pulled on my sleeve.

"What do you want?" I asked him.

He made his mouth go and tried to say something, but he still couldn't talk, so he couldn't say.

Then he started pulling on Ma's dress.

"What is it, John?" she asked, but he couldn't tell her either, so he grabbed Pa. He looked real frantic.

Pa looked surprised at John's making such a fuss.

"What's the matter, John?" he asked.

John opened his mouth, but still he couldn't make any words come out. His eyes got bigger and bigger. We could all see there was truly something wrong. Then, quick as scat, John let go of Pa and climbed up on the chair at the table. He turned over the picture of Bagley and began to draw fast on the back of the paper with his colored chalks. First a big arch, kind of wiggly, and I recognized it. It was like the bear cave in the picture book. Then he drew a sort of settee and a row of chairs.

"John," Pa said, "that's good, but we have to find Mr. Peterson."

All at once tears came down, which wasn't ordinary for John, so Pa hesitated to go. We all paid attention. John drew a big bear face. Only he didn't make the eyes with black centers in them the way he always did when he drew Bagley. He just left empty circles there.

John looked at Pa, but Pa shook his head. By now Pa was trying real hard to figure out what John was trying to tell us. We were all trying.

Then John squeezed his mouth tight shut and wiped his sleeve over his eyes. He took up a color again and started to print. It took a little longer than drawing.

Pa watched, and then read aloud, "Miss Mants help."

"By golly!" Mr. Schlaag shouted. "Pete Peterson was always chopping her kindling and taking in her wood and banking her stove. Maybe that's what he forgets. Maybe he went to go by Cora Mants! Only why wasn't he coming home? Did he got there? Or if he didn't got there, maybe three days she got no wood for a fire!"

He and Pa and William and Leland rushed out.

Miss Mants and the Meesong

I stared at the picture John had drawn. It was a bear cave, but it was Miss Mants's house too, with the chairs all lined up against the wall. Mostly I stared at what he'd printed: "MISS MANTS HELP."

"Dog" and "cat" and "bad" and "Jane" I figured he could have learned in school, but Miss Vordig for sure never taught him to print Miss Mants's name. I wasn't sure if they'd learned "help" yet either.

Ma and Katy and Caddie and Martha were looking too.

Maybe crying made his voice start to come back, or maybe he was getting better, because John whispered close to my ear, "The Meesong comes to the bear cave. The Meesong knows it's good."

"Is he saying how he knows Cora Mants needs help?" Ma asked.

"No," I told Ma. "He's talking about the Meesong."

It took me a while to explain about John and the Meesong. But the Meesong didn't have anything to do with Miss Mants, as far as I knew.

"I recollect as how Miss Mants said Pete Peterson brought in her wood, but I'd be surprised if John would remember that," I told Ma. "And I never told him how to spell Miss Mants's name. We only went to her house but once, and we haven't talked about her since."

I didn't know and John wasn't about to tell. He'd gone to the window Pa had cleared and was looking out with that straight ahead look that you knew he wasn't seeing the snow. Ma told him to come away from the cold window, but you knew he didn't hear her. Whatever he was seeing, he was plain star gone.

Ma put on her coat and boots and hat and scarf and mittens and got her snowshoes. "I'm going to the Petersons' and see that Ingrid and Billy are all right. I just hope Pete Peterson got to Cora Mants's house. You see to it that the fire doesn't go out." She lifted the lid on the wood stove and pushed in a log. If the fire went out, the water would freeze right in the sink.

"John, you come away from that window," she said again. "It's cold there. Katy, bring him close to the stove." Ma wrapped the loose-knit fascinator over her face to keep the cold from her nose and cheeks.

After she left, we sat around the stove. Katy wrapped a quilt around John and he fell asleep. She brought a pillow and laid him down across two chairs close by the heat.

I told Katy and Caddie and Martha more about the Meesong—how John said it took him places and knew everything and did everything better than anybody. Then we waited what seemed like forever, with one or the other of us going to the window every now and then to look.

We saw Arne Thorgeson with his big horses break through the drifts on the road. We saw Mr. Heldon, who has the lumber mill, go past on skis. We saw Joe Saint-Pierre go by with his horse and sleigh that usually has traps in the back. Finally we saw Joe's sleigh coming back with people in it. It came to our place, and Ma and Pa and Leland and William and somebody else got out.

Leland and William floundered through the snow on their snowshoes to the porch and took the sled back to Ma and Pa. Whoever it was got on the sled, and William and Leland pulled while Ma and Pa walked beside.

Well, then I saw it was Miss Mants.

In another minute we were all saying hello to her and helping her with her wraps. I should say that we were more than pleased to know she wasn't frozen. Katy asked did they have any word about Pete Peterson.

"Pete Peterson came to my house three days ago," Miss Mants said. "A good thing he did. I hadn't banked the fire properly and it had gone out during the night. Then I couldn't see to get it going again.

"I wrapped up in every blanket and quilt in the house. Even so, I'd have frozen if Pete hadn't got there. By then the storm was so bad he didn't dare leave. What was worse, he came down with the same fever little Billy had. He was almost off his mind with that and fretting over Ingrid and little Billy."

"You must be plain tuckered out, Miss Mants. Where is Pete now?" Caddie asked.

"He's home, and Ingrid's sister came by to help out," Ma told her. "Cora, you'll stay with us for a spell, and I won't take no for an answer."

I always wondered at Ma saying that, when she hadn't asked a question.

"You shouldn't be living alone," Ma went on.

Miss Mants shrugged. "I'll come to terms with that when it's time. It's not so easy to tolerate another body in the house when you're used to your own ways. There's nobody in town I favor to have around every minute. Anyway, you know well enough I haven't been altogether alone."

Ma looked surprised, and started to ask what she meant, when just then John roused up and saw Miss Mants.

We couldn't believe what he did. He went right to her, took her hand, and whispered, "I couldn't come to the bear cave."

Miss Mants put her hand on his head. Then, like she couldn't help herself, she stooped down and hugged him. "That's why I came here, John," she said.

We were all truly wordless, and even more so when John whispered, "It's good, the way you said. You'll see." He trotted off to hunt in Ma's catchall box, found what he was looking for, and came back to climb on his chair at the table. He began making pinholes in his picture.

Miss Mants sort of turned toward Ma and Pa.

"You don't know what a pleasure it's been for me to have John every day for an hour after school," she said. "Besides his

She stooped down and hugged him

learning so fast, I didn't know how alone I was before he came. I'll be forever beholden to you for sending him."

Pa's mouth dropped open, and Ma blinked like she does when she can't think what to say.

"You Bains all have minds of your own," Miss Mants kept on. "I expect Liza's giving Jane Vordig something of a time. She'll go on doing it until she's back in the fourth grade. You'd better have a talk with both of them. I don't doubt Liza's bored to tears where she is."

Ma and Pa looked at me and my underlip got tight.

They couldn't say a word though, because Miss Mants was still talking. "Just the way John is in school. You see, now and again there's a child with ideas and a way of thinking that are so different, a teacher hardly knows how to teach him. So she teaches the others the best she can, and there that child sits wondering what all this soft custard is when he's hurting for a piece of beef. John's one of those."

Ma looked doubtful. "It appears to us he's star gone most the time."

"Star gone?" Miss Mants asked.

"Woolgathers," Ma said.

"Always thinking of something else," Pa said. "He's forever doing that rather than paying mind to what he ought."

"We sometimes wonder if he knows what's pretend and what truly is," Ma said. "We were hoping school would shake him out of it."

"Only he's star gone there all the time too," I put in.

"Then there's this Meesong of his Liza tells us about," Ma said.

"The Meesong? Why, the Meesong has been the best thing there is!" Miss Mants said. "Shall I tell them, John?" She had a secret, smiley look, just like John's after he wrote "Jane is bad."

Everybody looked at John, where he sat putting pinholes in the paper. He nodded.

"He says yes, Miss Mants," I offered.

"The Meesong comes to my place every night," Miss Mants said, serious as could be. I knew by the look on Ma's and Pa's faces that they were thinking how peculiar she'd got. But Miss Mants couldn't see their faces, so she went right on.

"It tells me just what to have John do every day so he'll learn to write down what the Meesong knows. You might be surprised at what it's told him. And John is learning to write it all down. He's coming along so fast that the Meesong's having a hard time keeping up with the lessons."

Ma and Pa had less than nothing to say to that, so Miss Mants went on some more, sort of thoughtful.

"Star gone. I like that. The Meesong has taken John to stars most people won't get to in all their lives. Even when he's too big for the Meesong to keep him company, I expect John will go on visiting those stars—maybe forever. And he'll bring back pieces of them for the rest of us to savor."

I could see Ma and Pa were chewing on that when John slid down off the chair and put the paper in Miss Mants's hand. He'd only put holes in the letters, so he showed her where to put her finger underneath. She rubbed her fingers along slow and careful.

While she did, she said out loud, " 'Miss . . . Mants . . . help.' Why, John, that's just fine! Did the Meesong tell you to write that?"

John took his picture back and looked at the printing.

"No, I didn't need him," he whispered. For a minute he looked almost sad. Then he smiled. "I did it myself."

Miss Mants couldn't see him, I know, but she seemed to know through her skin how John was feeling. She turned toward Ma and Pa.

"Wouldn't you say it would be all right for him to be Stargone John so long as it doesn't interfere with his learning?" she asked.

"No harm that I can see," Pa said slowly.

Stargone John! With Miss Mants saying it the way she did, I figured it was good. So I'd not be so hard on Bradford Cronis for naming him forever. I might even find it in me to thank Bradford for bringing me the reader.

About the Author and Illustrator

Ellen Kindt McKenzie lives in the San Francisco Bay Area of California, but spends her summers in rural Wisconsin. Author of *Stargone John*, she has written other books for young readers, including *The King, the Princess, and the Tinker*.

William Low is an award-winning illustrator and a graduate of the Parsons School of Design. Illustrator of both *Stargone John* and *The King, the Princess, and the Tinker*, he lives on Long Island, New York, and teaches at Manhattan's School of Visual Arts.